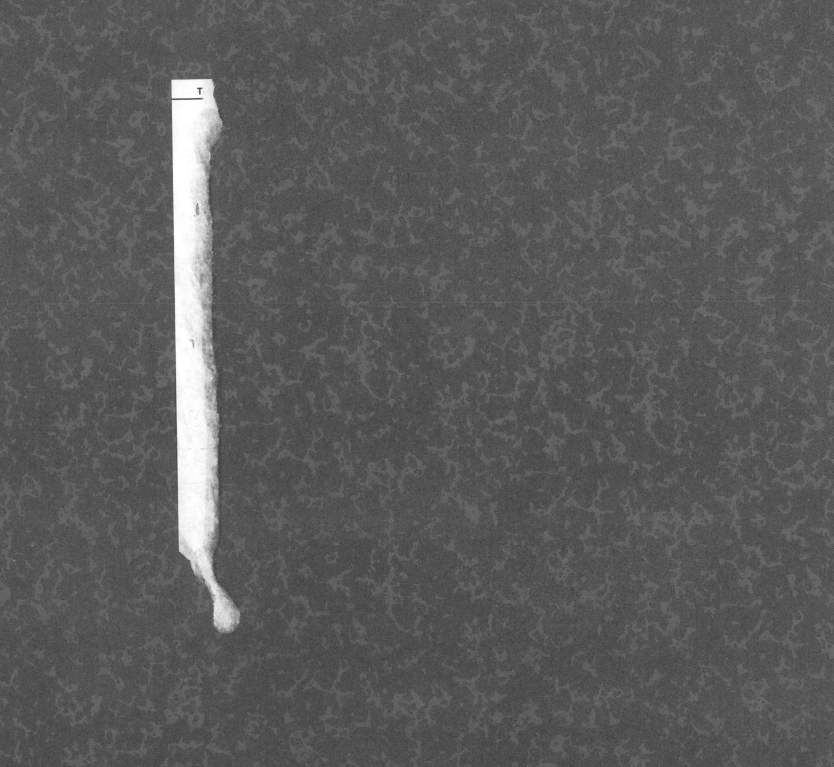

The Baby in the Hat

THE BABY IN THE HAT

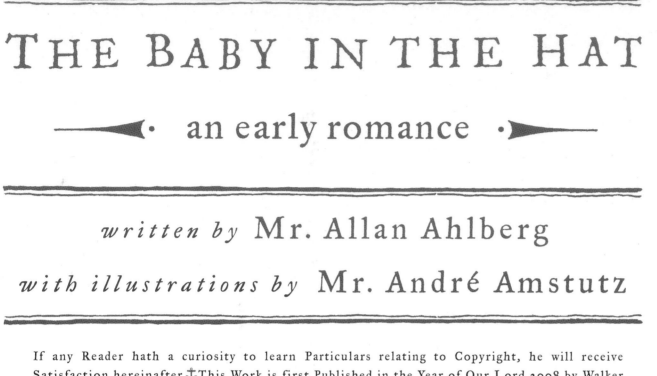

◄ • an early romance • ►

written by Mr. Allan Ahlberg

with illustrations by Mr. André Amstutz

WALKER BOOKS
AND SUBSIDIARIES
LONDON · BOSTON · SYDNEY · AUCKLAND

My Best Friend caught a Baby

In his Hat.

The Baby's Mother gave him
Half a crown.

He spent the money
On a Railway Ride.

Got lost in London,
Oh, the Fog was thick,
Fell off a bridge
And landed in a Ship.

Ahoy there!

Sailed down the river
To a Stormy Sea.

Became a Cabin Boy

And then — a Mate.

Engaged with Pirates
In the Southern Seas.

Served Good King William's Navy

'gainst the French.

My Best Friend then
A Captain he became,
With Loyal Crew
And Stout Ship of his own.

Then Home at last
With Treasure in his Trunk.

He walked that Street
Where he had caught the Baby,
A different, grander Hat
Upon his Head

And saw a smiling Face
Up at the window

And gave a Little Gasp ...

And fell  in Love.

My Best Friend
[I, his Best Man]
Soon was married.

His Bride — she was that Baby,

Did you Guess?

And now they sail
The Southern Seas together

With Loyal Crew and Baby

... of their own.

It's true!